In the great green room
There was a telephone
And a red balloon
And a picture of—

GOODNIGHT MOON

by Margaret Wise Brown
Pictures by Clement Hurd

Bunny
GOODNIGHT
MOON

The cow jumping over the moon

And there were three little bears sitting on chairs

And two little kittens
And a pair of mittens

And a little toyhouse
And a young mouse

And a comb and a brush and a bowl full of mush

And a quiet old lady who was whispering "hush"

Goodnight room

BUNNY
GOODNIGHT MOON

Goodnight moon

Goodnight cow jumping over the moon

Goodnight light
And the red balloon

Goodnight bears
Goodnight chairs

Bunny

Goodnight kittens

And goodnight mittens

Goodnight clocks
And goodnight socks

Goodnight little house

And goodnight mouse

Goodnight comb
And goodnight brush

Bunny
GOODNIGHT MOON

Goodnight nobody

Goodnight mush

And goodnight to the old lady
whispering "hush"

Bunny

Goodnight stars

Goodnight air

Goodnight noises everywhere

The Story of *Goodnight Moon*

Goodnight Moon is widely recognized as one of the all-time classic children's books. Its lilting rhythm soothes children to sleep, while the otherworldly artwork of Clement Hurd gives the book a magical quality not easily forgotten.

Margaret Wise Brown was a pioneer, a woman whose original approach to writing for the very young had a long-lasting impact on the world of children's literature.

Born in 1910 in Brooklyn, New York, from a young age Margaret defied convention. She preferred train sets and boats to dolls, and adventure fiction excited her more than the tame 'stories for girls' of the time. Margaret would read aloud to her younger sister, freely adapting the stories as she went to make them more exciting.

At college, Margaret gained a reputation as a free spirit, and generally preferred exploring outdoors to studying. But while there, she learned about the role of rabbits in folklore, including the mischievous Brer Rabbit from the Uncle Remus stories of the Southern United States, and the Moon Rabbit from ancient East Asian mythology, inspired by the rabbit-like shapes of the shadows on the moon's surface.

Margaret went on to train as a teacher. At the time, schooling in the United States was traditional and conservative: education was meant to prepare children for work. Margaret's training at the radical Bank Street school, however, focused on the needs of children – how did their minds develop, and the best of way of maximising each child's potential, regardless of their background. But while she liked spending time with children, she didn't take to teaching and longed to write stories instead.

Margaret's first book for children was *When the Wind Blew*, in 1937. Many more followed, and she also took up a position of editor in a publishing house. Margaret's approach was influenced by her own experience, and by a growing movement to try and reflect the real lives and minds of modern children, unlike the traditional fairy tales and nursery rhymes that had gone before. But although her own stories often reflected the way children really spoke and felt, they had a poetic, dreamlike feel, as well as her occasionally dark and surreal sense of humour (as demonstrated by "Goodnight nobody").

Goodnight Moon was the third book written by Margaret to be illustrated by Clement Hurd, an artist working in New York. Her illustration instructions were minimal, but she provided him with a reproduction of Goya's 18th century painting, *Red Boy*, as inspiration for the book's palette. Clement created several rounds of rough sketches, each of which was met with tough criticism from both Margaret and her legendary editor Ursula Nordstrom – the room didn't feel big enough, the old lady wasn't quite right. But slowly, the visual design came together.

Goodnight Moon was published in 1947 and sold well in its first year, but then sales began to decline. After Margaret's death in 1953, they began to grow again, until this unique and affecting book became a global publishing phenomenon – having now sold over 48 million copies worldwide.

Margaret did not live to see the extraordinary worldwide success of *Goodnight Moon*, but in her lifetime her books did sell many thousands of copies. Her life was adventurous and restless, but her work has brought peace and calm to the bedtimes of millions of children for more than 75 years.

Top tips for helping to get your child to sleep

by HANNAH LOVE, Sleep Consultant

Parents often see getting their child to sleep as a daunting problem to tackle. When parents contact me I reassure them that all children have the ability to sleep well – the most important thing is for the parent to stay relaxed, consistent and confident.

With that in mind and remembering that all children are different, here are my top tips for sleep:

- **Avoid short naps leading up to sleep time.** Even a "power nap" for a couple of moments could prevent your child from falling back to sleep for several hours!
- **"Sleep triggers" are key.** A good bedtime routine could include lullabies or white noise, a soft toy and a comforting book like *Goodnight Moon*.
- **Be realistic and have manageable goals.** If your baby is feeding to sleep don't expect you will move them instantly to falling asleep unaided. Choose a more gradual change and once your child is drifting off without feeding, you can look at ways of moving forward.
- **Bedtime should be a soothing time for everyone.** Children are amazing at picking up on your body language and tone of voice, so try to breathe deeply and talk softly – show that you're calm and they will find it much easier to unwind.
- **Reading should be the last thing you do before sleep**. It is best for the child to be fully ready for bed, with teeth brushed, before snuggling down with *Goodnight Moon* to get them fully settled.
- **Always prepare older babies and toddlers for change.** If you are embarking on any "sleep training" then explain the change you are going to make first – use role play or pictures to make it easy to understand.
- **Books can be one of the best aids to a relaxing bedtime.** Using the same book can be a good idea as children love repetition. The words should indicate that it is sleep time – this will help your child anticipate sleep approaching, which makes it seem less daunting.

Hannah Love (DipHE, DipION) is a sleep consultant, nanny, nutritional therapist, paediatric nurse and mother of three with over 20 years' experience of helping babies and children to fall asleep through her Yummy Baby Group.